Disney's TaleSpin

By Andrew Helfer
Illustrated by Sue Dicicco

A GOLDEN BOOK • NEW YORK

Western Publishing Company, Inc., Racine, Wisconsin 53404

Baloo and his little friend Kit were playing pinball at Louie's Place in Cape Suzette when a stranger came in. The fellow was out of breath and very excited. "You'll never believe what I just saw!" he gasped.

"Try me," said Baloo.

"I was out fishing on the other side of the island," the stranger said, "when my boat drifted into a foggy cove. Suddenly a huge ship appeared out of nowhere. It almost cut my boat in two! As it passed I could see an old bearded pirate standing on the deck. He flipped this coin at me—and then the ship disappeared!"

Louie came over and snatched the coin out of the stranger's hand. He held it up for all his customers to see. "It's a golden ragoon!" he said in awe. "But—that's impossible! All those ancient ragoons were stolen by the pirate Festus LeForge two hundred years ago, and his ship was lost at sea. . . ."

"Well, the pirate's back now!" the stranger said as he showed the coin to more of the customers. "And he's giving ragoons away! I'm going back for more!"

After the stranger left, the customers started talking about the gold ragoon. But one sly customer just sat and listened. He knew his boss, Don Karnage, would be interested in this tale of lost pirate treasure.

The story of the ghost ship spread quickly. Tourists came to Cape Suzette to see it. Louie told everybody he knew where the ghost ship would appear. "And for a dollar," he said, "I'll take you to see it!"

Louie led the tourists to a secret cove. Kit and Baloo followed. Kit watched as Louie set up a refreshment stand at the cove. "Something strange is going on here," Kit complained.

"You said it!" cried Baloo, pointing toward the ocean. "Look!"

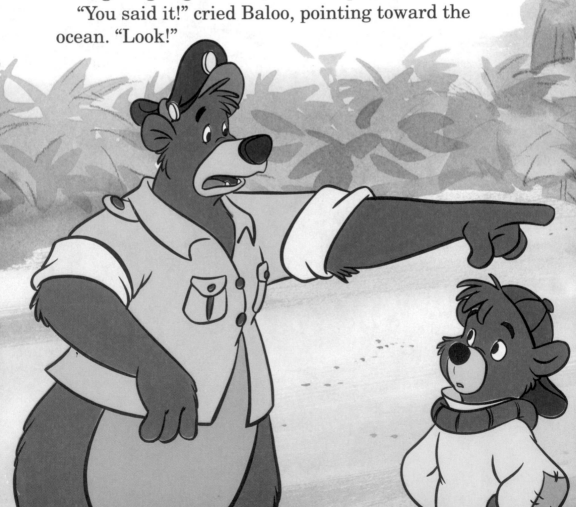

   From out of nowhere a thick fog had spread
over the water. No one could see a thing. And
then, from deep inside the fog, the ghost ship
appeared.
   The tourists gasped as an old pirate appeared
on the ship's deck. "I am Festus LeForge," the
ghostly figure said as he tossed a coin overboard.
It landed in the water with a splash.

"It's a golden ragoon!" one tourist cried.
All the tourists leapt into the water after the sinking coin.

Just then Kit and Baloo heard the sound of an
engine buzzing overhead. They looked up and saw
the *Iron Vulture*, the flying machine that belonged
to the dread pirate Don Karnage. As it flew over the
ghost ship, the *Iron Vulture* dropped a huge anchor.
It landed with a crash on the deck of the ghost ship.

"Uh-oh," Kit said. "I bet I know what's coming next. . . ."

With a mighty tug, the *Iron Vulture* pulled the ghost ship out of the water and lifted it high in the air.

"Ha, ha, ha!" a voice boomed from a loudspeaker in the *Iron Vulture*. "I, Don Karnage, am surely the greatest pirate of all time!" The *Iron Vulture* and its dangling cargo turned slowly to fly off.

"Come on, Kit," said Baloo. "Let's go after Don Karnage!"

Inside his flying machine, Don Karnage smiled. "Think of it!" he said to his crew. "I'm stealing treasure from the ghost of the greatest pirate of all time!"

"Man the controls," he told his men as he opened a hatch. "I'm going down to meet the great Festus LeForge personally!"

In a flash, Don Karnage slid down a rope to the ghost ship's deck. Sword in hand, he stood face-to-face with the old ghost pirate, who was trembling with fear.

"I've come for the golden ragoons, sir," Don Karnage said. "I shall fight for them if I must."

The old pirate reached for his beard . . . and pulled it off his face! It was the stranger who had found the first ragoon. "Louie isn't paying me enough to do this!" he shouted as he threw the beard to the ground. "I quit!"

Don Karnage was stunned. This was no ghost pirate! It was some kind of joke! And he had fallen for it.

Don Karnage was furious. He chased the fake ghost into the ship. Then he thought he saw someone else hiding behind some machinery.

"Another one of you?!" Don Karnage roared. In anger, he lifted his sword high into the air and smashed the machine. There was a hissing sound, and thick smoke began to pour out of the machine.

Not too far off, Kit and Baloo were racing toward the *Iron Vulture* in their plane, the *Sea Duck*. As it flew closer Baloo could not believe his eyes. The *Iron Vulture* was covered by a cloud of smoke. "Bet they're having trouble seeing where they're going!" Baloo said with a chuckle.

"They'd better turn quick!" Kit said. "They're heading straight toward the mountains!"

Baloo flew the plane over the ghost ship. Kit hopped out of the plane onto his airfoil and shouted a warning to the ghost ship crew.

On board the ghost ship, Don Karnage turned
and saw a huge mountain coming straight at them.
"PULL UP!" he screamed at the pilot of the
Iron Vulture. "PULL UP!"

It was too late for the ghost ship. WHAM! It smacked into the side of the mountain.

Kit was back safe inside the *Sea Duck* with Baloo. "Ow," he said as he looked back at the sight. "That must have hurt."

Don Karnage had grabbed the anchor rope just in time and was pulling himself up toward the *Iron Vulture.* "You did this on purpose!" he screamed up at his crew. "No one makes a fool of Don Karnage! You'll ALL walk the plank for this!"

Later, back at Louie's Place, Louie admitted to Baloo that the whole plan had been his idea. "I hired these two fellows to work with me. We fixed up an old ship and put a fog machine inside. I thought a ghost ship would improve business. But I hardly made enough money to pay for the fog machine."

"What about those gold ragoons?" Baloo asked.

"They weren't real, either," Louie said sadly. "Just wooden nickels and gold paint."

"Too bad," said Baloo. "I think those tourists want their money back!"